THE BLACK BOOK

VOLUME I

Some Other Titles from Falcon Press

Christopher S. Hyatt, Ph.D.
Undoing Yourself With Energized Meditation & Other Devices
Techniques for Undoing Yourself (CDs)
Radical Undoing: Complete Course for Undoing Yourself (DVDs)
Energized Hypnosis (non-book, CDs & DVDs)
To Lie Is Human: Not Getting Caught Is Divine
The Psychopath's Bible: For the Extreme Individual
Secrets of Western Tantra: The Sexuality of the Middle Path

Christopher S. Hyatt, Ph.D. with contributions by
Wm. S. Burroughs, Timothy Leary, Robert Anton Wilson et al.
Rebels & Devils: The Psychology of Liberation

Christopher S. Hyatt, Ph.D. & Antero Alli
A Modern Shaman's Guide to a Pregnant Universe

S. Jason Black and Christopher S. Hyatt, Ph.D.
Pacts With the Devil: A Chronicle of Sex, Blasphemy & Liberation
Urban Voodoo: A Beginner's Guide to Afro-Caribbean Magic

Antero Alli
Angel Tech: A Modern Shaman's Guide to Reality Selection
Angel Tech Talk (CDs)

Joseph Lisiewski, Ph.D.
Ceremonial Magic and the Power of Evocation
Kabbalistic Handbook for the Practicing Magician

Peter J. Carroll
The Chaos Magick Audio CDs
PsyberMagick

Phil Hine
Condensed Chaos
Prime Chaos

Steven Heller, Ph.D.
Monsters & Magical Sticks: There's No Such Thing As Hypnosis

Israel Regardie
The Golden Dawn Audio CDs
The Complete Golden Dawn System of Magic
The World of Enochian Magic (CD)
What You Should Know About the Golden Dawn

For up-to-the-minute information on prices and availability, please visit our website at http://originalfalcon.com

THE BLACK BOOK

VOLUME I

Principles of Extreme Living

Become Who You Are—There Are No Guarantees

by
Christopher S. Hyatt, Ph.D.

Illustrated by S. Jason Black

THE *Original* FALCON PRESS
TEMPE, ARIZONA, U.S.A.

Copyright © 2003 CE by Christopher S. Hyatt, Ph.D.

All rights reserved. No part of this book, in part or in whole, may be reproduced, transmitted, or utilized, in any form or by any means, electronic or mechanical, including photocopying, recording, or by any information storage and retrieval system, without permission in writing from the publisher, except for brief quotations in critical articles, books and reviews.

International Standard Book Number: 978-1-935150-37-4

First Edition 2003
First Original Falcon Edition 2008

Dedicated to Dave B on His 33rd Birthday
With Warm Regards to Jon Sellers

Address all inquiries to:
THE ORIGINAL FALCON PRESS
1753 East Broadway Road #101-277
Tempe, AZ 85282 U.S.A.
(or)
PO Box 3540
Silver Springs NV 89429 U.S.A.
website: http://www.originalfalcon.com
email: info@originalfalcon.com

The symbol you see was that of the "Extreme Individual Institute." Now that Dr. Hyatt is gone, the Institute is no more. Beware those who would assert otherwise! Beware the institutes and foundations and any other organization that purports to teach what Dr. Hyatt taught. Only Hyatt was Hyatt. No one else is, or can be.

The goal of the institute was simple: to assist extreme individuals to become who they are.

This work was for that 10% of marginal people who desire to become greater than they are now. It was not a forum or discussion or argument.

The methods of the Institute were simple: "work" in the arena of the obvious as well as the sublime. However, Dr. Hyatt was only concerned with results and not moralisms—what a person does with his power is his business.

Work was done individually via both personal contact and the internet, plus a yearly coming together done either in the physical or on the internet. There was a strict entrance exam and monthly payments were required for the operation of the Institute.

— Nicholas Tharcher

Principles of Extreme Living

DEATH IS AN ABSOLUTE
LIFE IS CONDITIONAL

All too many people are corks on the sea of life. They don't live life, they are lived by life.

The Extreme Individual Institute is dedicated to the proposition that many people can become creations of their own will for life.

Look at young children: they live life in wonder, excitement and joy. Our initial wonder, excitement and joy is defiled by parents and teachers.

The giggle must become the polite laugh, the fun must be only when appropriate, the spontaneity must be torn from our breast. Joy is replaced by drudgery and individuality surrendered to the social collective. Thus is life passed in stupidity.

As adults we can not begin anew, but we can take a solemn oath to recapture as much as possible of that joy, wonder and power we were born with.

To exist is easy—to live is an accomplishment.

We dedicate this little book to the those among you who are willing to live the full life.

We invite you to join with us in a journey into the wonder of life. To those we say: seas however high and a bountiful journey.

BECOME WHO YOU ARE—
THERE ARE NO GUARANTEES.

THE FIRST AND ONLY COMMANDMENT

First and foremost, seek your own welfare—your own enlightenment...

THIS IS IT!

Most people don't think, they simply repeat what they have been told. They substitute belief for argument and prejudice for thinking. Accept nothing that someone tells you unless it is provable—most people don't think—they have random thoughts and live like zombies

All assertions of infallible knowledge are false. Your own knowledge is your only guide —you need no one's permission to be stupid or smart.

In fact, there is no one to give you permission. The first great error is believing there is someone who can.

There is no one to protect and preserve you—simply no one.

And if you don't want to follow this commandment, there is no one who cares.

Life is all too short when it is enjoyed; life is all too long when it is suffered.

Keep in mind that what we are presenting is not for hair-splitters; that means psychoanalytical institutes or castrated academics who need to consult the oracle before they can make a move...... we are writing for people of action who do not require 100% proofs or guarantees.

**BECOME WHO YOU ARE—
THERE ARE NO GUARANTEES.**

THE FOUR NOBLE TRUTHS

All is stupidity ……

The cause of stupidity is the structure of the human brain…… It is the brain of the slave and not that of a self-determined being. Human beings are their own enemies.

The cure is brain-change willed.

If you are capable—stand above and beyond the outcry of the fool. Just say no—to stupidity.

The method is the eight-fold path.

BECOME WHO YOU ARE—
THERE ARE NO GUARANTEES.

THE EIGHT-FOLD PATH
RIGHT UNDERSTANDING

Do no harm to anyone unless it is necessary—it is dirty work and time consuming—be swift—Annihilate Karma.

Do not steal from others, Teach them to give you what you want.

Sex is pleasurable—however it has been turned into sorrow. Lust is the result of culture and childhood—Lust is not proof of your value—It is proof of your being owned.

Do not lie unless it is beneficial to you.

Do not make up stories—unless you can sell them.

Do not use mean language—unless it is called for…and then be devastating.

Do not say more than is necessary unless you are being paid.

Do not preoccupy yourself with other's toys unless you can convince them to give them to you.

Do not bear ill will—just do it and get it over with.

Avoid wrong views such as altruism and collective religion. All that keeps you safe is you—your wishes will not save you, only reality can do that.

BECOME WHO YOU ARE—
THERE ARE NO GUARANTEES.

Right Mindedness

Avoid all obsessions.

Anxiety is a tool for learning about your own weakness.

Guilt is the acid of life—if you think you are guilty of something either correct it or forget it.

Don't harbor thoughts of ill will. do them or drop them.

Do not obsess over thoughts of revenge, just take your revenge when the time is right.

Keep away from life wasters—cultivate yourself.

BECOME WHO YOU ARE—
THERE ARE NO GUARANTEES.

RIGHT SPEECH

Avoid lying unless it is to your advantage and you will not get caught.

Avoid making up stories about yourself or others unless they increase your power.

Be gentle and kind until it is time to be mean. and then strike with no mercy.

Avoid mindless talk. Be mindful of your words and note their effects.

BECOME WHO YOU ARE—
THERE ARE NO GUARANTEES.

RIGHT ACTION

Be sympathetic concerning the welfare of others as long as it benefits you. Do no harm unless absolutely necessary — then be a vampire — This requires patience and skill.

Take nothing from anyone, let them give it to you...... put them in your debt...... only take if you have been taken and then take everything.

Avoid sexual relations with idiots, morons and the severely emotionally disturbed. if you do not abstain, disappear as quickly as possible. do not get emotionally involved with them.

You are better off masturbating... Most relationships are simply diversions from facing the void.

In order to say "I love you" you must first have an "I." Few do.

Always act like you are a person on an expense account.

BECOME WHO YOU ARE—
THERE ARE NO GUARANTEES.

Right Living

Discipline your life.

Go above and beyond the smiling, sneering monkey called your neighbor.

Keep your Honor and your integrity—keep clean—avoid clutter.

Avoid owning useless things.

Set your own goals and then go after them. Goals are chosen. Use them to serve you and do not become the slave of your goals. When conditions change, your goals can also change.

Eat right, exercise, keep away from losers.

BECOME WHO YOU ARE—
THERE ARE NO GUARANTEES.

RIGHT EFFORT

Avoid stupid people and ideas...... If an idea doesn't make sense, throw it out. If a technique doesn't work, flush it.

Overcome failure and mistakes. Cut your losses—learn without self abuse.

Maintain your status but be subtle. Make yourself into a piece of art, but do not be ostentatious...... Do not lower yourself for anyone or anything unless there is a great gain.

Loyalty to yourself is essential. Loyalty to a profession, a job, a company or a teacher is secondary.

***BECOME WHO YOU ARE—
THERE ARE NO GUARANTEES.***

RIGHT ATTENTIVENESS

Attend to your body.

Attend to your feelings.

Attend to your mind.

Attend to your surroundings.

Attend to your benefit.

Set and seek your own goals.

Attend to your own enjoyment. If others also enjoy, that is a benefit; but your own enjoyment and gain is the objective.

BECOME WHO YOU ARE—
THERE ARE NO GUARANTEES.

Right Concentration

Stay focused on your goals.

Do not get lost in possessiveness—learn to let go of junk. Sell it at a profit or sell it at a loss, but don't stay on a train going in the wrong direction.

Treat life like a poker game. Luck only counts when it is mixed with the utmost focus and skill.

An unfocused thought is a contradiction in terms.

Death is defined as brain death. If you are not thinking clearly, you are the walking dead, a zombie.

BECOME WHO YOU ARE—
THERE ARE NO GUARANTEES.

*BUT JUST IN CASE YOU MISSED THE POINT*É

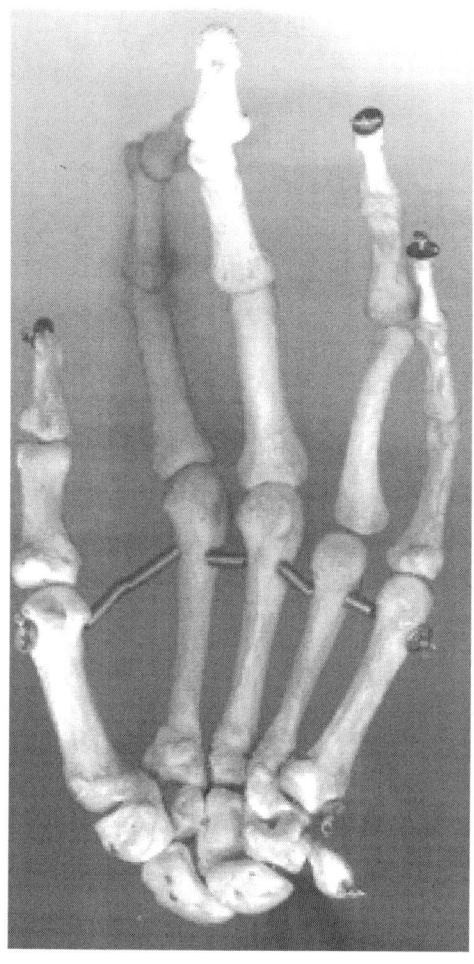

In the face of death, decay and disease, we quote Silenius, "what is best for human beings is utterly unattainable: not to have been born, not to be, to be nothing. But the second best is to die soon."

If you are reading this we offer our condolences and our best wishes for a successful future.

BUT YOU ARE HERE—NOW—SO—

Live life as a journey of personal pleasure. When it is time for it to end you should be able to look back with a smile. If you know that you are to die one hour from now and you can not review your life with pride and satisfaction, then you have changes to make. No choice is without cost, but the highest cost is to "live" a meaningless life.

***BECOME WHO YOU ARE—
THERE ARE NO GUARANTEES.***

PRINCIPLES OF EXTREME LIVING

DEATH IS AN ABSOLUTE
LIFE IS CONDITIONAL

All too many people are corks on the sea of life. They don't live life, they are lived by life.

The Extreme Individual Institute is dedicated to the proposition that many people can become creations of their own will for life.

Look at young children: they live life in wonder, excitement and joy. Our initial wonder, excitement and joy is defiled by parents and teachers.

The giggle must become the polite laugh, the fun must be only when appropriate, the spontaneity must be torn from our breast. Joy is replaced by drudgery and individuality surrendered to the social collective. Thus is life passed in stupidity.

As adults we can not begin anew, but we can take a solemn oath to recapture as much as possible of that joy, wonder and power we were born with.

To exist is easy—to live is an accomplishment.

We dedicate this little book to the those among you who are willing to live the full life.

We invite you to join with us in a journey into the wonder of life. To those we say: seas however high and a bountiful journey.

BECOME WHO YOU ARE—
THERE ARE NO GUARANTEES.

THE CAUSE—!
THE CAUSE—?[1]

---

[1] "The Cause—The Cause" was originally penned circa 1965–66 in Hollywood, California. This was the time of the great—often misguided—freedom revolution. In comparing that period to the results which have followed, freedom—as well as liberty—have lost more ground than we care to imagine.

Dr. Hyatt lost the original document but not before it was published in a now defunct *avant-garde* journal based in New England. The only similarity to this piece is the title, the spirit and the author.

> *Those who can make you believe absurdities can make you commit atrocities.*
> — *Voltaire*
>
> *Whatever the tyrant doesn't steal belongs to the Church.*
> — C.S. Hyatt, in a lighter moment.
>
> *It has been said that man's body belongs to the tyrant, his soul to the Church—but both drink his blood from the same cup.*
> — C.S. Hyatt, in a even lighter mood.

I propose that enough time has been spent on suffering. Instead I posit that man's fear to live in the infinite luxury of life is the prime root of his misery.
But what is The Cause?

Why is man so fearful of abundance?
Abundance is unpredictable—out of society's control. And what is society?
It is the fortress by which the whole planet has gone mad.
But what is it? Where did it come from?

Society—culture—is a wonder story—it is a story for the walking dead.
Is this The Cause?

Is man a malignancy searching for the Cause of himself?

The fortress society is built on shifting sands.
This is the great joke: the more society tries to be in control, the weaker it becomes.
Watch this society crumble as it tightens the screws on the citizen.

Serfdom is the ultimate standard. Is it the Cause?
"Obey, be safe, don't stand out" is the cry.
Have we found The Cause yet?
Each and every society has and will destroy itself.
The Cause?

Remember ancient Rome—it killed itself by fostering mediocrity.
It did this by destroying the Cause. Is this the Cause?
Kill the unique and free individual.
The Cause—The Cause.
So the great ones went underground.
Is this the Cause?

What was Rome's new face?
Pity—
But even Pity has not found the Cause?

Society is—what?
God in disguise?
But what is man's problem?
An Itch?
Scratching for The Cause?
The way we describe "reality" creates problems which demand answers which create more problems.
Is this The Cause?
We are taught that if we feel discomfort or pain something must be done and this something must be Done—Now.
Don't stop the pain—
Find the Cause.
Find the Cause—Now!

We must find the culprit—
"The Cause—The Cause"
The We must find it.
We must find the Culprit—
The Cause—but never is it found—
never in its purity.
Why?
The Cause—The Cause
IS?

His DNA?
His most sacred creations?
His Gods?
His society?
The Cause, The Cause……
The Cause must be found!

Police Cause—
Cause Casters—
Laws Cause—
Leaders Cause—
Cause Causes—
And from these we have Cause Libraries—
strangled Causes—
One Nation Under Sheep
With liberty and justice
For WE.

Do you want to find out what to do?
Consult Dead Causes—you will find the answer.
If not, elect a new Cause—
Blind Ballot—but find that Cause.
Lift the Sheets,
Look under the Bed.
In the Closet.

Caste the bones
the Cause
The Cause—The Cause

But the Cause is Man
his creations—
so kill the Cause—
put an end to It,
Not guns
Not sex
Not loss of values
Not criminals
Not freedom
Not liberty
Not stem cells
Not abortions
Not science
Not drugs
Not queers
Not Etc.
Not Cod.
But man himself.

Simply Kill the Man.
Man is at fault—the Cause.
Why?
He is evil.
Who says so?
The invention—God-Society.
He Dis-Obeyed the first Cause,
just Kill Him and get the Cause.
The Cause—The Cause
is in the Sauce.

Something has to go—either man or the Cause
but something has to go—so Kill IT.
Or maybe just Kill—
freedom,
the neighbor,
the wife,
guns,
sex,
satan,
liberty,
intelligence,
science,
reason—
Kill your pet Cause
everything will be better
—but what if the Cause is YOU?

Every idiot knows The Cause
—the jew
the negro
the queers
the devil
the kids
the oil
the dow jones.
Poverty
clothes,
drugs,
porno
abortion.
IT is the Cause
just Kill IT.
Now……

Or return to the past—
which past?
whose fiction—?
how far back shall we go
—to the Garden?
the Dark Ages?
Atlantis?
return return
to family values—?
which ones—I pray.
it doesn't matter—just return—to where—?
—the Cradle?
Look to psychology,
look to jesus,
look to the Oracle,
look at the screen,
just keep looking.
Daddy Please
Daddy Please
Please Find

the Cause
the Cause—

Where is it hiding?—
In the Grave—
The Cause—The Cause—
somewhere
sometime, but always—look—
When you find it
just Kill IT,
hang it,
burn it,
shoot it,
gas it,
poison it—but quick—
for the Cause must die—Now.

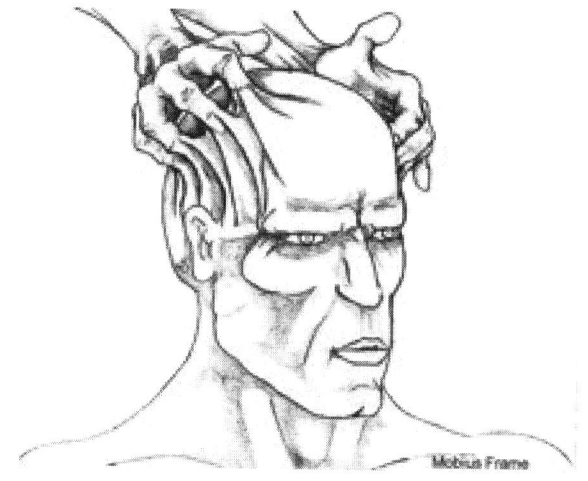

But how can man live without The Cause?
How can he live without the Sauce?
He can't.
So let us Invent and Invent we have—
God in his Studio—
God in His Sauce—

God setting His books—
God
Cod—the Idiot's Higher Power,
forever lurking,
lurking
lurking
Softly lurking
under her chamber door
searching for porno
in the little girl's scribbles
a remarkable achievement to be born?
—masturbating behind the closet door—
Please Daddy
Don't let me come again
Oh Daddy
Big Daddy
Oh! Big Daaadddeeeeeeee

Off to God
Off to AA
Off to the wedding bed.
Off to the CIA
Under the Gun—
Under the white Cloak
but please Daddy
find it, find it daddy, Please
Before I come again.
The Cause
The Cause

God the Father—Pay TV.
God the Son—Kill Bill.
God the Holy Ghost—Matrix DNA.

But where is IT Daddy?
the cause, the cause.

a cause
be cause
cause cause
da cause
he cause
r cause
me cause
she cause
the cause
they cause
we cause

Cause—The Wizard of Oz cause—
because of the wonderful things He does.
The Cause—The Cause

There is a need to know
but only
the Cause Knows
only He knows
not She knows
but only he knows
what He knows
not you
not me
Only He—the We Knows
Count
Three for You
One for Me.......
Eight for We

We, yes!
We the Ghost
the holy host
knows
The Cause

God Please Help me
find the Decoder Ring
I want more Ovaltine.

The Cause—The Cause

PREVIEW OF UPCOMING ACTION

We could not end this first **Black Book** without briefly mentioning the single most significant flaw in the human brain, the most significant error in our nature.

(A full discussion of this subject will be presented in a subsequent publication by The Extreme Individual Institute. Here we will provide a glimpse.)

There is, in all human beings, a compulsion to repeat.

We spend our life compelled to repeat the traumas and conditions of our childhood because we believe we can change them. This process is automatic.

We believe that we can change what already has happened.

We repeat the traumas; we repeat the conditions in different situations and guises.

No one is immune from this condition—no—one. Differences between people are simply a matter of degrees.

We can not undo the past, but more importantly we can't undo the feelings, thoughts and conditions of the past.

Keep in mind that our early thoughts and feelings have been contaminated by our youthful imagination.

Those incidents where you were shamed, felt weak, helpless, anxious, terrified, defeated, humiliated or brutalized are continually being repeated in the present, in an attempt to undo them. Though this sounds absurd, it is true.

The original incidents and failed repetitions have since governed our life in more ways than you can imagine.

There is only one answer to this past: simply accept it. This means that some of these unpleasant feelings will live with you until the end, but do not focus on them. Switch your attention from the past to what is happening now and what you are capable of doing.

No matter what you do now you will not undo those original events or feelings.

Live with it and move on. However, you must first become aware of how you are repeating the past; the patterns, the forms, the situations and the conditions. This is the most difficult task.

Strive for power in the now—for the present and future only. You can use past pain and failures for motivation—but remember it will still not undo the past. For example if you have a lot of hate, learn how to transform it into success, power and wealth.

Many individuals in an attempt to undo the past will attempt to alter their mood state through chemicals, and compulsions of all types. This will not work.

Others will attempt to do the opposite of what they grew up with thus defining themselves in the negative.

But regardless of what you try, you can't alter the historic facts.

Children are inherently narcissistic. This is not bad or a flaw. It is what drives them to attempt to walk, to dress themselves, to throw and catch a ball, to excel in sports or academics. Narcissism is partially responsible fro developing social relationships.

When the child's narcissism is crushed or deeply wounded—it does not matter whether maliciously or innocently—the resulting damage haunts that child throughout his adulthood and he tries to recover it historically by re-enacting the situations in the present.

There is no completely satisfactory solution to this human condition. There is a way to reduce the effect.

Accept the truth, the finality, the actuality of those early traumas . Accept defeat. accept that you did not have control over the situation at that time. No Blame—no Fault.

It is only when you accept the finality of the past injuries that you can begin the difficult journey to extreme individualism and getting all that awaits you now.

BECOME WHO YOU ARE—
THERE ARE NO GUARANTEES

THE *Original* FALCON PRESS

Invites You to Visit Our Website:
originalfalcon.com

At our website you can:

- Browse the online catalog of all of our great titles
- Find out what's available and what's out of stock
- Get special discounts
- Order our titles through our secure online server
- Find products not available anywhere else including:
  - One of a kind and limited availability products
  - Special packages
  - Special pricing
- Get free gifts
- Join our email list for advance notice of New Releases and Special Offers
- Find out about book signings and author events
- Send email to our authors
- Read excerpts of many of our titles
- Find links to our authors' websites
- Discover links to other weird and wonderful sites
- And much, much more

Visit us today at originalfalcon.com

Made in the USA
Middletown, DE
10 September 2024